A New Handwriting for Teachers

This edition published 2025
By Living Book Press
147 Durren Rd, Jilliby, 2259

Copyright © Living Book Press 2025

ISBN: 978-1-76183-018-1 (softcover)
       978-1-76183-020-4 (hardcover)

First published in 1907

A catalogue record for this book is available from the National Library of Australia

A NEW HANDWRITING

for teachers

by

M. M. BRIDGES

THE Accompanying plates are intended chiefly for those who teach Writing: a few words, both of apology & explanation, are needed to introduce them.

I was always interested in handwriting, & after making acquaintance with the Italianized Gothic of the sixteenth century, I consciously altered my hand towards some likeness with its forms & general character. This script happening to please, I was often asked to make alphabets & copies, & begged by professional teachers to have such a book as this printed, that they might use it in their schools. One can never quite satisfy one-self in the making of models for others to copy, but these plates are very much what I intended, though, owing to my inexperience, some of them have suffered in the reproduction.

The best facsimiles are the first two pages—the capitals—which were cut in wood by James D. Cooper, from a reduced photograph. The copperplate alphabet of small letters & the copperplate sentence, 'All the ways,' plates 3 & 6, were unfortunately not photographed, with the result that the engraver's curves are too mechanically rounded, & some of the forms have lost their character & have approached the uniformity of the common copybook hand: this is specially the case with the letters b, c, g, h, m, n, o, as will be seen on comparison with the three pages of free writing at the end of the book. These last—plates 7, 8 & 9—are true facsimiles, except that they had to be printed faint, to disguise an apparent shakiness of the downstrokes, due to my having unfortunately written on a finely-ribbed paper.

Plates 4 & 5, which are collotypes, are also exact facsimiles.

No. 10 is from a MS. in the Record Office, of the date of Edw. VI: the method of reproduction does not do justice to its forms, but it has only to be copied with a free quill for its beauty to reappear.

No. 11 is a reproduction of the facsimile of Michael Angelo's careful handwriting in Guasti's edition of his works. There can scarcely be a better example of Italianized Gothic. It shows individual forms, which are well worth studying.

Following the preface will be found instructions how to use the copies; it will be seen that for young beginners I give simplified forms & the order in which it is convenient to learn them. A child must first learn to control his hand & constrain it to obey his eye: at this earliest stage, any simple forms will serve the purpose; & hence it might be further argued that the forms are always indifferent & that full mastery of the hand can be as well attained by copying bad models as good; but this can hardly be: the ordinary copybook, the aim of which seems to be to economize the component parts of the letters, cannot train the hand as more varied shapes will: nor does this uniformity, exclusive of beauty, offer as good training to the eye: moreover I should say that variety & beauty of form are attractive, even to little children, & that the attempt to create something which interests them, cheers & crowns their stupendous efforts with a pleasure that cannot be looked for in the task of copying monotonous shapes.

But whether such a hand as that here shown lends itself as easily as the more uniform model to the development of a quick, useful cursive, I cannot say; & it is possible that the degradations, inevitable in the habit of quick writing, might produce a mere untidiness, almost the worst reproach of penmanship. Some of the best English hands of to-day are as good a quick cursive as one can desire, & show points of real beauty; but such hands are rare & are only those which have, as we say, character; which probably means that the writer would have done well for himself under any system: whereas the average hands, which are the natural outcome of the old copybook writing, degraded by haste, seem to owe their common ugliness to the mean type from which they sprang: & the writers, when they have occasion to write well, find they can do but little better & only prove that haste was not the real cause of their bad writing.

It is certainly desirable that there should be more good models for slow writing, as there is abundant occasion for its use; & in providing models it seems to me better to offer modern scripts, the product of to-day, rather than to attempt to resuscitate an ancient one however beautiful: & this is really the only excuse for my attempt, for there are of course plenty of beautiful models of various dates: it would be a good thing if reproductions of these, such as have been published by the Palaeographical Society, were hung in our schools, not only to give to children the history of their own Alphabet, but also to show them how lovely a thing handwriting can be.

M. M. BRIDGES.

INSTRUCTIONS
HOW CHILDREN SHOULD
USE THE COPIES

*W*RITE *on ordinary 'sermon paper,' which is ruled with faint lines about ⁵⁄₁₆ of an inch apart, making the short letters the height of a space. It is important that pens, ink & paper should consort well: a pen that suits one paper writes ill on another, or with different ink. Generally speaking, a fairly yielding, broad nib, as a J, a broad 'ladies" pen, or quill, with freely flowing ink, on intermediate paper, neither rough nor smooth, works best.*

Enough has been written & said about the position of the hand in writing: I would only recall the old traditional rule of two fingers on the pen, which seems to have been founded on experience & not without reason: & also insist on thick downstrokes: any thickness in the hori-zontal part of the stroke betrays a wrong position of the pen.

The capital alphabet is given first in the book, but children begin of course with the small letters, & the fourth page will show the order in which it is most convenient to teach these: the simple strokes of which the letters are composed should be first learned, & after each stroke the resultant letters, which, on this page, are simplified for the beginner. When these are mastered, the more varied & difficult forms of the third page can be learned. In this small alphabet, a few of the letters have two or three variant forms: in some cases these are merely alternatives & can be used according to taste; others are for distinct use, as initials or finals, &c.

The variants are as follows:—

> d: the second is only for use as a final; i.e. at the end of words: see page 5.
>
> e: three forms of this letter: the first is begun from below & is to be used when following a letter which ends with a stroke rising from below, such as h: see he on page 5: the second e & third e follow letters the last stroke of which ends high; the third e is made in two strokes; see be & oxen on page 5.
>
> f: the two forms can be used indifferently, but see of on page 5.
>
> j, k, p, q, z: either form of these five letters may be used, but the first form in every case implies a careful & somewhat ornamental style, & the simpler forms are better for quick writing.
>
> s: the nearer the small s keeps to the form of the capital the

better, but it becomes modified when joined with other letters: the way to join it will be found on page 5.

t: either form may be used at pleasure.

v, w: the first form given of each of these letters can only be used to begin words: see vow on page 5.

x: how to join this letter, see oxen on page 5.

The double letters are only suggestions, but such small varieties add interest to the appearance of manuscript.

Of the capitals, where there could be any doubt as to how they are to be formed, I have shown the construction on page 5: in the case of B, D, E, M & Q, the black line indicates the first stroke: the dotted, the second.

At the end of the capital alphabet will be found a few alternative forms. A, D, the first E, F, O, P & T may be useful as being written in one stroke. The second alternative E, though necessitating three strokes, can be made very quickly by one continuous flowing motion of the pen, see page 5, where the whole passage of the pen is shown by the line which it would make if not raised off the paper. The alternative S is optional.

On page 5 I have given a set of Arabic numerals.

The copperplate 'All the ways of life,' which follows, shows the letters, without modification, combined into words, & it may be used as a copy:

but it should be remembered, as pointed out before, that the curves are too much rounded by the engraver.

The next three plates, 7, 8 & 9, will show what the script is like when it approaches a current hand. They are in fact reproductions of the hand, which it is the object of this book to teach; any one who adopts it will, knowingly or unknowingly, modify it, & it must not be considered as the only possible or indeed best outcome of the forms on which it is founded.

Plates 10 & 11 will give other choice of forms, and may be studied or copied.

A B C D E
F G H I J K
L M N O
P Q R S T

U V W

X Y Z

A D E E F

O P S T

2

a b c d d e e e f f

g h i j j k k l m n

o p p p q q r s s t t u

v v v w w w x y z z

ff ſ g g th st a œ &

STROKES	LETTERS	STROKES	LETTERS
l l	i t u	o	o
ı	r	c	c e
ı	n m	o	a d
l	h p f	u u	q j g
l	l b	k	s x
v	v w		y z z

4.

1 2 3 4 5 6 7
8 9 0

B D L M

Q B

and. he. be. of. joy.

vow. oxen. so. is.

5.

All the ways of life are pleasant;
in the market place are goodly
companionships & at home griefs
are hidden; the country brings
pleasure, seafaring wealth, &
foreign lands knowledge.

Come & sit under my stone pine, that
murmurs so honey sweet as it bends to
the soft western breeze ; & lo this honey
dropping fountain, where I bring sweet
sleep, playing on my lonely reeds —

Thyrsis, the reveller, the keeper of the nymphs
sheep, Thyrsis who pipes on the reed like Pan,
having drunk at noon, sleeps under the shady
pine, & Love himself has taken the crook &
watches the flocks

7

Read not to contradict & confute,
nor to believe & take for granted,
nor to find talk & discourse, but
to weigh & to consider.

Some books are to be read only in
parts; others to be read, but not curious
ly; & some few to be read wholly, &
with diligence & attention

Bays yield no smell as they grow, rosemary little, nor sweet marjoram ; that which, above all others, yields the sweetest smell in the air, is the violet ; especially the white double violet, wh. comes twice a year - about the middle of April, & about Bartholomew-tide. Next to that is the musk rose ; then the strawberry leaves dying, with a most excellent cordial smell ; then the flower of the vines _ it is a little dust, like the dust of a bent, wh. grows upon the cluster in the first coming forth; then sweetbriar, then wall-flowers

Cum itaq rogor de dante & prebete corpus & Sanguinem domini
id est, vivificam horum totiusq Christi Communionem: dico
Christum, qui in medio Sacror est, cuiusq hec verba sunt
Accipite & Manducate, Principem & efficacem datorem esse
scripsisse, ministrum autem ita ei ad hanc sui prebitionem
ministrare, sicut ad eam quam Euangelio prebet, & baptismate
propter quod ministrum. Paulus recte scripsit se Corinthios
domino per Euangelium genuisse, & Christum ipsorum cordib
inscripsisse, & galathas parturiisse:

Si vero de usu hic panis & vini rogor, Respondeo Signa esse
exhibitiua, quib Dominus ita sese exhibet & prebet, sicut
discipulis prebuit Spiritum Sanctum Signo afflatus oris sui,
& sicut tactu manus multis contulit Sanitatem corporis &
mentis, Sicut visum luto facto & sputo, Sicut Circumcisione
Carnis, Circumcisionem Cordis, Sicut Baptismate regeneratione.

Fide paterna dei Charitatis erga nos vinim vitam aeternam.
Hec fides committur, alitur & prouehitur, quod Christus filius
dei, se & meritum omne suum donat nobis, vivitq in nobis,
peccatoq liberatos excitabit a mortuis in vitam perfecte beatam
& coelestem. Proinde Cibi & Potus, Symbolis voluit dominus hic
uti, & dare Carnem suam manducandam Spiritualiter, symbolo
panis manducandi corporaliter: Et Sanguinem suum bibendu
spiritualiter, Symbolo vini bibendi corporaliter. Eandem enim
ut dictum est dat sui Communionem in Coena per Symbola &
verba sua quam commendauit Jo. 6. tantum verbis.

Si roger, qua possit esse comnectio gloriosi corporis Christi existetis
in coelis et certo coelor loco, cum Pane corruptibili contento
in terra et loco sensibili: Respondeo, ea que est regenerationis
cum tinctione aqua, & que spiritus Sancti cum afflatu
oris Christi. Pacti coniunctionem esse dico, ut qui fide vera
unaq communicat hijs Signis corporaliter, spiritualiter
vere percipiant confirmationem et Incrementa communi=
onis corporis & Sanguinis domini, eius, qua sunt membra
Christi. caro de carne eius, Os ex ossibus eius. Vt fiut
hec perfectius.

Dal ciel discese e col mortal suo poi
che visto ebbe l'inferno giusto e'l pio
ritorno vivo a contemplare dio
per dar di tutto il vero lume a noi

Lucente stella che co raggi suoi
fe chiaro a torto el nido ove nacqu'io
ne sarel premio tutto'l mondo rio
tu sol che la creasti esser qui questo puoi

Di dante dico che mal conosciute
fur l'opre sue da quel popolo ingrato
che solo a iusti manca di salute

fuss'io pur lui catal fortuna nato
per l'aspro esilio suo cola virtute
dare del modo il piu felice stato